The Angel and Other Stories

The Angel and Other Stories

Retold by
Sue Stauffacher

Illustrated by
Leonid Gore

Eerdmans Books for Young Readers
Grand Rapids, Michigan   Cambridge, U.K.

Text © 2002 by Sue Stauffacher
Illustrations © 2002 by Leonid Gore
Published in 2002 by Eerdmans Books for Young Readers
An imprint of Wm. B. Eerdmans Publishing Company
255 Jefferson S.E., Grand Rapids, Michigan 49503
P.O. Box 163, Cambridge CB3 9PU U.K.

Stauffacher, Sue, 1961-
The angel and other stories / written by Sue Stauffacher: illustrated by Leonid Gore.
p. cm.
Summary: Retellings of folktales which reflect Christian oral traditions from fifteenth
and sixteenth century Europe.

ISBN 0-8028-5203-3 (alk. paper)

1.Christianity–Folklore. 2. Tales–Europe. [1.Christianity–Folklore.
2. Folklore–Europe.] I.Gore, Leonid, ill. II. Title.

PZ8.1.S7887 An 2002
398.2–dc21
2002021614

The illustrations were rendered in acrylic paints and pastels on paper.
The display type was set in Cataneo Light Swash.
The text type was set in Caslon 540.

To my grandmother, Irma Grace Stauffacher,
whose deep faith is an inspiration.
— *S. S.*

For Elizabeth, Mark, and their parents.
— *L. G.*

Table of Contents

The Shepherd's Prayer

On the edge of a vast desert in a hollow that protected him from the bitter wind, a young shepherd boy brushed clear a space beside his fire, tucked two new lambs against his bony breast, and settled down to sleep. Leaning back on the earthen pillow he had fashioned, the child gazed up at the vast expanse of glittering heavens and sighed.

"Oh God," he said with great feeling. "If you were a lamb, I would warm you beneath my cloak. And if you were caught tight in the thorny bush, I would leave my flock to aid you. For that's how much I love you.

"I tell you, God, if you had a sore foot I would carry you upon my shoulders and if your muzzle was full of cactus needles, I would remove them slowly so that you would not feel the pain too dearly."

The child continued on in this manner for some time.

"If you were a fallen bird, dear God, I would weave you a nest of ocotillo branches and feed you nectar from the saguaro blossom, for that's how much I love you."

Reaching out to his meager stack of firewood, the shepherd tossed another stick onto the dying fire. He added a handful of dried sage to sweeten the smoke.

Then a terrible thought occurred to him. What if God were a hungry coyote?

As if sensing this turn of mind, the young lambs stirred and began to bleat. The shepherd boy let them suckle his fingers. When they had quieted, he said, "If you were a hungry coyote, God . . ."

He broke off, listening to the wind that swept over the little hillock where he lay. "If you were a hungry coyote, dear God, I would give one of my lambs to feed you. For that's how much I love you."

Now, it so happened that a wandering scholar was crossing the same desert where the shepherd boy offered his prayers to God. Surprised to hear the sound of a human voice so far from any village, the scholar paused to listen to the child's speech.

But when he heard this final prayer, the scholar rushed over to the boy and said, "My dear child, this is no way to pray. God, a hungry wolf? You will offend the All Mighty with such a comparison."

The boy wrapped the lambs in his cloak and invited the scholar to come sit beside his fire. He gave the old man a drink from his goatskin pouch and shared what was left of his simple meal.

Then he sat back and waited patiently for the scholar to finish, for he, too, was hungry, hungry for instruction in the ways of the world. Growing up by himself in the desert, the child had never been taught the correct way to worship God. Simple prayers were all he had to offer, fashioned as they were from the fullness of his heart.

The child bent close to the fire and examined the scholar's belongings as the old man spoke at some length about lighting candles and preparing the ground for worship. He showed the child scrolls full of strange marks like animal tracks that the boy did not understand. He stood and kneeled and clasped his hands in what seemed a confusion of movement.

When he finished, the old man drank again from the shepherd's precious supply of water.

"This is how to honor God," he told the child sternly. "Praying is a

discipline for which you must devote a good part of each day in practice."

From that day forward, the little shepherd prayed no more. He was ashamed of the prayers he had said before he met the scholar. In his desire to share the fullness of his heart with God, he said only what came to his mind. Why would God All Mighty wish to know the thoughts of a simple shepherd boy who could not even read or write?

The scholar continued on his way. By day he shared the word of God, and in the evening he slept the deep sleep of the righteous. But one evening he had a most disturbing dream. In the dream, his candles were melted, his prayer scrolls torn and scattered to the winds, his hands unable to clasp themselves in prayer. A whirlwind arose, stinging his face with sand and clouding his vision.

And from the maelstrom came a voice, a deep resonant voice, a voice that did not need to raise itself to be heard, for it was the voice of the All Mighty himself.

"You would deprive me of the innocent prayers of a child?" the voice asked the scholar.

"Never," responded the scholar.

There followed a silence as deep and black as a starless night.

Plucking up his courage, the scholar continued. "I teach the word of God so that man and child alike will sing his praises."

"And yet," responded the voice, "my little shepherd prays no more. Of all the prayers from all the corners of the earth I have loved the little shepherd's prayers the most, for though he had no knowledge of the world and had committed no great deeds, he thought to do good with all his heart.

"Teach him not the error of your ways," the voice commanded, "but rejoice in the goodness of his."

The next morning, the scholar gathered together his candles and his scrolls and set out to retrace his path. When at last he found the young shepherd, he spoke warmly to the child and asked if he might spend the night in his company.

The young shepherd now welcomed the stranger as a friend. Again they shared a simple meal together, and when it came time for them to go to sleep, the child spread his cloak on the ground for the old scholar.

"Shall we pray?" asked the scholar.

The child did not answer, but looked past the scholar into the dancing flames.

"Perhaps you would like me to pray for both of us," the scholar said, "since I am so wise."

Nodding his head, the child replied, "That would be best."

So the scholar lay down on the child's cloak. He gazed up at the brilliant stars and sighed.

"Oh God, if I were a shepherd, I would speak to you from the fullness of my heart," he said. "And I would let no one, not a coyote or a lamb or even a foolish old man, come before my love for you."

The child stared at the scholar who did not light any candles. Nor did he read from any scrolls.

"I would tell of newborn lambs and of the tender grasses that grow by mountain streams," the scholar continued. "If you were cold in the night, I would wrap my cloak around you, dear God. And in the day, I would shelter you from the burning sun. These things and more I would do for you, God, for that's how much I love you."

"And if you want to be silent, God," began the young shepherd, "I will sit beside you in silence. And if you are sad, I will play you a tune on my flute . . ."

"Yes, yes, dear child. This is how you must pray forever," said the old scholar. "For though I have traveled many miles upon this earth and studied with the great masters, it took a young shepherd boy to remind me that the Merciful One always seeks the heart."

~ from Micha Joseph Bin Gorion

Péquelé

There was once a poor performer named Péquelé who lived off the small fairs that traveled from village to village, springing about like a squirrel on the little mat he placed in the market square. Heaven knows what acrobatics he launched into, leaping about like a monkey, somersaulting, walking on his hands, tying himself into knots like a snake and then untying himself again.

I say he lived, but he didn't live well. People always look down on those who wander about the countryside. For them, work is growing wheat with the strength of their arms. Each day they struggle with brambles and thistles. They can hardly give much thought to traveling entertainers. Poor Péquelé did not see many coins fall upon his carpet.

He now knew only by rumor what a roast of beef might be or even a nice steaming bowl of thick soup. As pale as a church candle he was, and as thin as the draft in a keyhole. But he roamed on, leaping and dancing, hair in his eyes, like a wet cat.

His spirits were high, but after a time his body was no longer willing to accompany them. One December evening at nightfall, Péquelé stumbled in some brambles and collapsed a few paces farther on at the base of a roadside cross. There he fainted.

Happily, two begging friars on the way home to their cloister found him just as it was beginning to snow and loaded him on their donkey. At the monastery he got some wine to drink and some hot soup. The next day he tried walking again, but his legs were all rubbery and wouldn't hold him. The abbot said he could stay a week to get his strength back.

The week went by and the snow melted. The south wind cleared the roads.

"My good friend Péquelé," said the abbot. "All friends must part. We're going to fill your pack so you can set out on the road again."

"If you please, Father Abbot," returned Péquelé, "I'd rather stay here."

"Ah, but our rule won't let us keep a passing traveler more than three days," said the abbot. "You'll come again next year, and we'll give you three days on retreat."

But poor Péquelé remembered the good round bread on the table, the bowls filled with lentils, and the chunks of cheese washed down with a little wine. The peace of the abbey reminded him of a room with a fire in which you sit, watching the snow outside.

How miserable it is — compared to this — to live on the open road! The wind whistles, the rain beats in your face, and the dogs people loose at the sight of you bark savagely and snap at your heels.

But there was still more in the monastery to capture the heart of poor Péquelé. Ever since he was a tiny boy doing somersaults in the grass, he'd loved Our Lady and had given her his heart. There, before her image in the cloister's beautiful chapel with its red and blue stained glass windows, he felt closer to her than anywhere else in the world.

"Oh please, Father Abbot, won't you keep me so I can be a friar with the others?"

"Do you think Our Lady needs an acrobat in this monastery?" asked the abbot sternly. "It's true you're good at somersaults, but that's all."

Péquelé hung his head. One tear after another fell down his cheeks.

"All right," said the abbot after a moment. "But you must promise me you'll be a good monk, and worthy of the name."

"Oh yes, yes, Father! I so love the Holy Virgin!"

"You may stay as novice. In three months time, we shall look into the matter further."

Péquelé shone with happiness. Carried away by joy he flipped upside down, walked on his hands, then turned cartwheels round and round the chapel. Nothing like that had ever been seen in the room before.

"Enough, enough, Péquelé! We'll overlook your frolicking this once. But now you're a novice, and this must never happen again. Do you understand, Péquelé?"

"I understand, Father."

"No more leaps and somersaults!"

"Absolutely not. No, no."

"You're going to put on the habit and stop acting like a carnival buffoon! Are we agreed?"

"Yes, Father Abbot, agreed!"

Péquelé had promised with all his heart, like a child. And with all his heart he kept the rule three days, three weeks, and three months. But winter was past now and spring was coming. Soon the snowflakes sailing by on the wind would be changed to petal blossoms of hawthorn and plum. Already he could hear the blackbird, the first to sing at the spring thaw. Far off, in the heart of the woods, the cuckoos called forth yellow flowers to bloom in the grass.

Something got into Péquelé's legs — something like the mad melody of a flute played by an energetic child.

The abbot, who saw everything, knew that Péquelé had springtime in his veins.

"Listen, my son," said he, "your work for today is to prune the orchard. Get up there in the tops of the apple trees and take out all the dead or weak branches."

So Péquelé got up in the trees, his pruning hook in hand. Here and there he hopped, like a tightrope dancer. And all at once, in the spring wind, he discovered he was lighter than down. He ended up leaping from apple tree to apple tree like a squirrel.

When he got to the end of the orchard, of course he had to come down and put back on the habit he'd taken off for climbing. But first, on the grass in his shirt and breeches, all alone, free and full of fun, he just couldn't resist. Off he went, standing on his head, walking on his hands, doing leaps and twists and flip-flops of all sorts, filling the orchard with acrobatics as a goldfinch fills its cage with song.

The abbot came to check on Péquelé's progress and saw everything.

Péquelé promised very humbly never to do such a thing again. No more somersaults, oh no! In fact, he apologized so sincerely that the abbot couldn't help relenting. He sighed a big sigh and drew his hands back into his sleeves.

"Very well," he said. "I'll keep you on probation awhile longer. But if you don't keep your promise, out you go!"

The abbot thought the problem was springtime in his veins, did he? No, it wasn't so much that as a heartfelt joy. Some evenings, Péquelé's heart was just bursting with joy.

The weather was fine, cool, and bright with a nice breeze. The setting sun, as red as a red-hot iron, was turning the air in the distance all pink. You could see a few circling birds, the blue countryside settling into evening calm, and all space opening to the peace of God.

Poor Péquelé thought he didn't know how to offer up dignified prayers like the other monks. But somehow he had to thank the Lord who made all things so beautiful. And it seemed to him that he could do this by doing the one thing that he was good at in all the world — the tricks of a showman and a carefree child.

The abbot called the other monks together. The matter seemed settled even before the conversation began. The monks simply could not shelter in their monastery a monk who leaped about like a goat.

"Surely, he's no great sinner," said one kind monk, speaking up in Péquelé's defense.

"Ah," replied another. "But recall the somersaults, the cartwheels, the handstands. It's what he was born to do. It's what he's known all his life. He can't help it."

"It's true that we haven't been able to mend his ways," said the abbot sadly. "I'm afraid he's still a madcap. And no madcap will ever be a monk."

Péquelé confessed his fault and wept. He could not defend himself. After all, it was too true. But the thought of leaving his pretty white room and Our Lady's beautiful chapel made the tears stream forth, just like the spring at the back of the orchard.

The abbot, his eyes on Péquelé, felt a quiver in his stomach. More than one friar was close to tears and so was he. But this rash action, this catapulting from tree to tree seemed just too outrageous to let pass. Péquelé hadn't managed to progress on the wise and sober path of a monk, so he would have to tread his old path, that of an acrobat, once again.

They stripped off his habit and gave him back his mat and his pack.

The abbot excused himself immediately and went to pray in the chapel.

"I had to do it," he kept repeating. "Poor Péquelé's still a child. And we, Our Lady's servants, can't be romping about like children any more."

He was immersed in such thoughts, when from a dark corner he heard a slight noise. Not far away, Péquelé was unrolling his mat on the chapel's flagstones. He was right in front of the statue of the Virgin Mother.

"Our Lady Mary," said Péquelé. "I wanted to live in your house all the days of my life, but as you can see I'm not worthy. Still, I mean to thank you for the time I've spent here almost as your little boy."

Believing himself alone in the chapel, he addressed Our Lady as volubly

as a child. And what did he do next but start in on his tricks. Bending and stretching, rolling and leaping, he did every trick he knew, but with so much spirit, so much soul, that the abbot, who was about to get up and stop the whole thing, stayed right where he was.

Suddenly, Péquelé stood motionless, bathed in a dazzling light. He had come down on his feet, his face streaming with sweat and almost breathless. And at that very moment — the abbot saw it happen — the Virgin left her stone pedestal and came to Péquelé on a ray of light. She leaned over him and with the edge of her veil gently wiped his moist forehead.

Like a mother caressing her child, she caressed the strolling acrobat. The chapel was ablaze with light.

"Forgive me, Our Lady, forgive me," murmured the abbot, bowing his head to touch the rail of his stall. "I thought I was truly wise, and yet I could not see wisdom. What do we really know, after all, except to gather at your feet like children, innocently and with joy? That's all the saints have ever known — to love God with all their heart, and God's Mother, and everything that is of God. This strolling acrobat is a greater saint than us all."

Péquelé stayed at the monastery to pray and to do his leaps and tricks, which in spirit were easily worth any prayers. Then, one fine day, he died. They say Our Lady appeared at his bedside and the abbot saw her there. Just as she had that evening in the chapel, Our Lady leaned over her poor acrobat to wipe away with her shining veil the sweat of his exhaustion.

~ from Henri Pourrat

The Angel

"When a good child dies, an angel comes down from heaven and gathers the child in his arms. Then the angel spreads his wings and flies with the child to visit all the places that the little one has loved. They pick a whole armful of flowers and bring them to God. In heaven, these flowers will bloom even more beautifully than they have on earth. God presses all the flowers to his heart; but to the one that is dearest to him, he gives a kiss, and then that flower can sing and join in the hosanna."

This is what one of God's angels was telling a dead child swaddled in his arms as he carried him to heaven. The child heard it as though in a dream, while the angel flew with him above all the places where he had played and been happy. At last they came to a garden filled with the most beautiful flowers.

"Which ones shall we take along and plant up in heaven?" asked the angel.

There was a tall rosebush whose stem some careless hand had broken, so that all the branches with their half-opened buds had already begun to wither.

"Oh, the poor bush!" cried the child. "Take it along that it may flower again up with God."

The angel kissed the child for the choice he had made and took the rosebush. They picked other flowers, too. The child loved the wild pansies and violets just as well as their elegant neighbors in the garden.

"Now we have enough flowers," said the child. "Now we are ready to fly up to God!"

"Yes, yes," the angel nodded, but still he waited. Night came, and the town grew still. The angel flew with the child above the narrow streets where the poor lived. The day before had been moving day, and the lanes were filled with old straw, broken pots and plates, rags and garbage.

The angel pointed to a broken earthenware pot. Near it lay a dried-out wildflower, to whose roots a clump of soil still clung. It had been thrown out in the street together with the other trash.

"That flower we shall take along," said the angel. "And I shall tell you its story while we fly." The angel picked up the dead wildflower and they flew on their way.

"Down in that narrow street," the angel began, "there lived in a cellar a little poor boy. He was ill from birth, poor creature, and had spent his life in bed. When he was 'well,' he would walk around the room, leaning on two crutches. In the middle of the summer, when the sun was so high in the sky that its rays fell into the little courtyard, a chair would be placed by the door of the cellar, and there the boy would enjoy the warm sunshine. The child had to hold up his hands in front of his face, for his eyes were used to the twilight of the cellar. His hands were white and thin, and beneath the transparent skin one could see the blood pulsing through his veins. After such a day his parents would say, 'Today he has been outside.'

"He knew about the greenness of the forest in spring because the neighbor's children would bring him the first green branch of the beech tree. The sick boy would hold it over his head and pretend that he was out in the woods where the sun shone and the birds sang. One day one of the children brought him a bouquet of wildflowers. Among them was one flower that still had roots. This was planted in an earthenware pot and placed next to the bed.

"By some miracle it grew. Each year new shoots and new flowers

unfolded. The wildflower became the sick child's garden, his treasure on this earth. He watered it and took care of it, making sure that it always stood where the bit of light that came through the tiny cellar window would fall upon it. The flower became part of his world, not only when he was awake but when he dreamed as well. It bloomed for him alone, to give pleasure to his eyes and send sweet fragrance for him to enjoy. When God called him, the boy turned in death toward the flower.

"He has been with God a year now. A whole year the flower stood in the window forgotten. By then it was all dried out so it was thrown out in the street with the other garbage. We shall take the poor dead flower along in our bouquet for it has spread more happiness than the grandest flower in any royal garden."

"But how do you know all this?" asked the child whom the angel was now rushing toward heaven.

"How do I know?" the angel asked, and smiled. "I was myself that sick little boy who could not walk without crutches. Oh, I recognize my flower again!"

The child opened his eyes as widely as he could and looked into the happy face of the angel. Just at that moment they flew into heaven where all sorrows cease. God embraced the dead child, pressed him to his heart, and the child grew wings and flew away, hand in hand with the angel who had brought him into heaven. God pressed all the flowers that they had given him to his heart.

But the dead wildflower alone he kissed. It gained a voice and could sing with the angels that flew around God in ever widening circles out into infinity.

All sang with equal bliss — those who had died when old and those who had come as children and the little wildflower that had been thrown out with the trash in the dark and narrow lane.

~ *from Hans Christian Andersen*

Where Love Is, God Is Also

Martin the shoemaker lived in the city, in a basement room with one window. The window looked out onto the street. Through it Martin would glance up and watch the people passing by. Only their boots were visible, but Martin had lived so long in this place and repaired and sewed so many shoes and boots that he could often recognize their owners as they passed by.

He was a faithful workman who used good material and charged a fair price. All his life he'd been a good man, but as he grew old Martin began to think more and more about his soul and how he might grow nearer to God. His wife had died long ago, and none of his children had survived him. In his grief, Martin had turned to the Bible.

After some time, life became quiet and joyful. In the morning, Martin would sit down to work until he finished his allotted task. Then he would take the little lamp from the hook, get his Bible from the shelf, open it, and sit down to read. And the more he read, the more he understood, and the brighter and happier his heart grew.

Once, in the deep of winter, it happened that Martin read late into the night. He was reading the Gospel of Luke, the sixth chapter. He was reading these lines: "*Give to every man that asketh of thee; And as ye would that men should do to you, do ye also to them likewise.*"

He read further and came to the story of the woman who had annointed

his feet and with her own tears and kisses had welcomed the Lord. And Christ was more moved by her than by the rich man's banquet.

"How should I have welcomed him?" Martin wondered, as he drifted off to sleep.

"Martin!" Suddenly his own name sounded in his ears.

"Who is here?" He turned around and glanced toward the door — no one.

"Martin," came the voice again. "Look tomorrow on the street. I am coming."

Martin arose and rubbed his eyes. He did not know if he had heard those words in a dream or while awake. He turned down his lamp and went to bed.

In the morning he rose, made his prayer to God, lighted the stove, and put on cabbage soup and gruel and water to make his tea.

As he gazed out his window, Martin saw an old man with a shovel. It was old Gregor.

"Hmmm. I must be getting crazy in my old age," thought Martin. "I thought Christ was coming to visit, and it is just old Gregor, pausing before my shop."

He studied the old man, who was warming himself and resting. Evidently, Gregor did not have strength enough even to shovel the snow.

Martin cracked the window. "Gregor," he called. "Come in. Warm yourself a little."

"May Christ reward you for this," said Gregor. "My bones ache."

"Don't trouble to wipe your feet," said Martin. "I will clean it up myself. Let's have a cup of tea." He poured hot tea into a cup for Gregor and a little into the saucer for himself.

Gregor stretched his frozen fingers around the cup and sipped gratefully. The two men sat in silence. Gregor finished and turned his cup on its side, but Martin snatched it up again.

"Drink some more for your good health," Martin urged him.

When they had finished, Gregor arose and said, "Thanks to you, Martin, for treating me kindly and satisfying me, soul and body."

"You are welcome. Come again. Always glad to see a friend."

Gregor departed and Martin poured the rest of the tea, drank it up, sat down by the window, and returned to his work. He was stitching a patch in a pair of felt boots, but kept looking up, for he was expecting Christ. All the while he was thinking of him and his deeds.

Two soldiers passed by, one in boots that Martin had sewn, and then the baker with his heavy basket hanging low. All hurried on, but one woman who stopped near the window. She had on homemade boots and woolen stockings, but the rest of her garments were meant for the summer. She had stopped to pacify a child. Martin could hear it crying loudly.

He leapt up, opened the door, and cried, "My good woman! Why are you standing in the cold with that child. Come into my room where it is warm. This way."

The woman was astonished. She saw an old, old man in an apron calling to her. She followed him inside, and he motioned her over to sit on the bed.

"Sit down there and get warm," he said. "Then you can nurse the little one."

"I have no milk for him," she said sadly. "I myself have eaten nothing since morning."

Martin brought out cabbage soup and bread and laid a towel on his little worktable.

"Sit down and eat while I mind the little one. I had babes of my own once, you see."

The woman crossed herself, sat down at the table, and began to eat. Martin took a seat on the bed near the infant, smacking and smacking to it with his lips, but the infant continued to cry. Martin ladled a little of the gruel he'd prepared earlier onto a spoon and began to feed the child while the woman told him who she was and where she was going.

"I am a soldier's wife. It is now seven months with no tidings since they sent my husband off. I lived as a cook, but when the baby was born, no one cared to keep me with a child. I wanted to engage as a wet nurse — no one would take me. I am too thin, they say."

Martin sighed and said, "Haven't you any warm clothes?"

"This is the season for warm clothes," said the woman. "But just yesterday, I pawned my shawl for a twenty kopek piece."

Martin stood and rummaged through his cupboard, drawing out a heavy coat.

"Ah, it's an old thing, but take it," he said. "You may turn it to good use."

The woman looked at the coat and burst into tears. "May Christ bless you, Grandfather! He must have sent me to your window, for we would have frozen to death if not for you."

"It is true I have been at the window all day," said Martin. Then he told the soldier's wife his dream and how he had heard the voice of the Lord promising to visit him that day.

"All things are possible," said the woman. She rose and wrapped her little child in the coat and went to the door.

As she passed out of sight, Martin saw an old apple woman with a heavy basket come to rest at the building opposite. Suddenly, a young lad in a torn cap came around the corner, picked up an apple, and was about to make his escape when the old woman caught him by the sleeve. She grabbed the youngster by the hair, scolding him and threatening to call a policeman.

"Let him go, Babushka," Martin called out, hurrying up to them.

And to the boy, "I saw you take the apple. Ask the Babushka's forgiveness, and don't you ever do it again. I will pay for this," he said, and took an apple from the basket and gave it to the boy, who eyed it hungrily.

"You ruin them that way, good-for-nothings," said the old woman. "He

ought to be beaten so that he remembers it for a whole week."

"That is according to our judgment, but not to God's," Martin said quietly. "If he is to be whipped for an apple, then what ought to be done to us for our sins?"

The boy burst into tears and began to ask forgiveness.

"That's so," said she, "but the trouble is boys like this are very much spoiled."

"Then we who are old must teach them." Martin pressed a few coins into the woman's hand as she regarded the boy thoughtfully.

"A childish prank, maybe," she said, lifting her heavy basket to her shoulder once again.

"Let me carry it, Babushka," said the boy. "It is on my way." And side by side they passed by Martin's shop. And Martin returned to his work in the waning light and finished up his chores. He swept up the cuttings, cleared the table, lit the lamp and ate a bit more of his soup. He took down his Bible and recollected last night's dream and his foolish notion that Christ himself would visit that day. It was then that a voice whispered in his ear:

"Martin, did you not recognize me?"

"Who?" exclaimed Martin.

"Me," repeated the voice. "It was I . . ." and Gregor stepped forth from a dark corner and vanished just as quickly.

"It was I," said the voice and the soldier's wife appeared, smiling down at her child.

As she vanished, the woman and boy appeared as if in a dream. "It was I, Martin."

Martin's soul rejoiced. He put on his spectacles and began to read the Evangelists, where the book happened to fall open.

"I was thirsty and ye gave me drink. I was a stranger and ye took me in . . ."

And further down, *"Inasmuch as ye have done it unto one of the least of these my brethren, ye have done it unto me."*

And Martin understood that his dream had not deceived him. The Savior really had called on him that day, and he, Martin the shoemaker, had received him.

~from Count Leo Tolstoy

The Star Child

It was winter and a night of bitter cold when two poor woodcutters made their way home through a great pine forest. The snow lay thick upon the ground and upon the branches of the trees. As they reached the outskirts of the forest, a strange thing occurred. There fell from the dark night a bright and beautiful star. It did not burn out, but continued earthward and seemed to sink behind a clump of willow trees.

"Why, there's a crock of gold for whoever finds it," they cried and ran eagerly through the brush. There was indeed a parcel of gold lying on the white snow, wrapped in a cloak of golden star-covered tissue that glowed warmly as if woven from filaments of light. As the men kneeled down to unwrap their treasure, they found inside, not gold or jewels, but a small child fast asleep.

"This is a bitter end to our hope," said one to the other. "Let us leave it here. We are poor men with children of our own."

"I am as poor as you," said his companion. "But it is an evil thing to leave an innocent child to perish. Let us bring it home, and I will deliver it into my wife's care."

His wife did not rejoice when she heard the news.

"Our own children lack bread, and you wish to give it to another? Who takes care of us? Who will find us food?"

"None but God who cares for the sparrows even and feeds them."

"Do the sparrows not die of hunger in the winter?" she asked, but held out her arms for child.

"It is a Star Child," he answered her and told her the strange manner of its finding. His wife unwrapped the golden cloak and her eyes filled with tears at the sight of the sleeping babe.

So the Star Child was brought up with the children of the woodcutter. He ate at the same table and played the same games. And every year he became more beautiful to look at, so that all those who lived in the village were filled with wonder.

For, while the children of the village were swarthy and dark-haired, his skin was luminous and his curls like the ringlets of a young lamb. His lips were like petals of flowers and his eyes like violets by a river of pure water. Yet his beauty was an evil spell cast upon him, for he grew up proud and cruel and selfish.

He teased the children of the village, saying that they were poor and he noble, being born from a star, and he made himself master in their games and called them his servants. He had no pity for the poor or for those who were blind or maimed, but would cast stones at them and bid them beg their bread elsewhere.

Often the woodcutter and his wife would scold him, "We did not deal with you this way. Why are you so cruel to those who deserve your pity?"

The priest of the village tried to teach him love of living things, saying to him, "The fly is your brother. Do it no harm. The wild birds are free. Do not snare them for your pleasure. God made the worm and the mole, and each has its place. Who are you to bring pain into God's world?"

But the Star Child did not heed the priest's words and would laugh at him in front of his companions. The children followed him, for he was fair and fleet of foot and could dance and pipe and make music. Wherever the Star Child led, they followed, and whatever he asked them to do, they did. They laughed when he pierced the eyes of the mole with a reed. And when he clipped the wings of the wren, they laughed also.

Now there passed through the village one day a poor beggar woman. Her garments were torn and ragged, and her feet were bleeding from the rough road on which she traveled. Being weary, she sat down under a chestnut tree to rest.

The Star Child happened by and saw her and called to the other children, "There sits a beggar woman. Look how ugly she is! Let us drive her away." And so the children came near and threw stones at her and mocked her.

Did she flee? Did she raise her arms to protect herself from the stones they cast? No, she did nothing but gaze sadly at the Star Child.

The woodcutter was not far off, and when he saw all that had happened he began to scold the Star Child.

"Surely you are hard of heart to torment this poor woman so. What evil has she done to you that you would treat her this way?"

The Star Child grew red with anger and stamped his foot upon the ground and said, "Who are you to question me what I do? I am no son of yours and will not do your bidding."

"What you say is true, but I showed you pity when I found you in the forest, did I not?"

When the woman heard these words she gave a loud cry and fell into a faint and had to be carried to the woodcutter's house where his wife revived her. But she would not eat or drink what was set before her, only fought back tears as she asked, "Did you not say you found the child in the forest? And was it not ten years ago from this day?"

The woodcutter stroked his beard, reflecting.

"And was there not around him a cloak of gold tissue embroidered with stars?" she asked, growing excited. When the woodcutter drew it from the chest, she wept for joy and said, "He is my little son whom I lost in the forest. I pray send for him quickly, for in search of him have I wandered over the whole world."

So the woodcutter went out and called to the Star Child, and said to him, "Go into the house, and you will find your mother waiting for you."

The child ran in, filled with wonder and great gladness. But when he saw who was waiting there, he laughed and said, "Where is my mother? I see none here but the vile beggar woman."

The woman answered, "I am your mother."

"You must be mad," cried the Star Child angrily. "I am no son of yours, for you are a beggar, and ugly, and in rags."

"But you are indeed," cried the woman. "It was robbers who stole you from me and left me to die. But I have recognized you and have named your cloak of golden stars. I pray you, come with me for I have searched the world over for you and I have need of your love."

The woman wept bitterly, but the Star Child hardened his heart against her.

"If in truth you are my mother, then it would have been better that you stayed away and not come here to bring me shame. Go away from me now. I do not wish to see you again."

"Will you not kiss me before I go, for I have suffered much to find you?"

"I would rather kiss the toad in the ditch or the slithering snake than such a foul looking woman as you."

So the woman rose up and dragged herself off into the forest and the Star Child returned to play with his friends. But when they beheld him coming, they mocked him and said, "You look as foul as a toad, as ugly as a snake. Get away from us." And they drove him from the garden.

The Star Child frowned and took himself off to the well to see what the children meant, and there, in the water's reflection, he saw that his face was indeed the face of a toad and his body scaled like a snake. Then he flung himself down in the grass and wept and said, "Surely this has come upon me by reason of my sin, for I have driven away my own mother. Now I must go and seek her

31

through the whole world. Nor will I rest till I have found her."

So he ran away into the forest and called out to his mother to come to him, but there was no answer. All day long he called to her, and when the sun set he lay down to sleep on a bed of leaves. The birds and the animals fled him, for they remembered his cruelty and he was alone.

In the morning he rose up and plucked some bitter berries from the trees and ate them and stumbled through the great wood, asking anyone and anything he met if by chance they had seen his mother.

He said to the mole, "Can you go beneath the earth and tell me is my mother there?"

And the mole answered, "You have blinded me. How should I know?"

He said to the wren, "You can fly over the tops of tall trees and can see the whole world. Tell me, can you see my mother?"

And the wren answered, "You have clipped my wings for your pleasure. How should I fly?"

The Star Child wept and bowed his head and prayed forgiveness of God's things and went on through the forest. When he passed through the villages the children mocked him and threw stones at him, and the farmers would not suffer him even to sleep in their silos for fear he might bring mildew on the stored corn. There was none who had pity on him.

For three long years he wandered over the world. He often seemed to see his mother on the road in front of him and would call to her and run after her till the sharp flints made his feet bleed, but he could not overtake her. He grew weak and sickly and often lay down by the side of the road, and even so none had pity on him.

One day, as he reached the outskirts of a great wood, the Star Child heard from a thicket a cry of pain. Forgetting his own sorrow, he ran to the place and saw there a little hare caught in a trap left by some hunter.

The Star Child had pity on it and released it gently.

"You have given me my freedom," said the hare. "What do you wish in return?"

"Only my mother," wept the Star Child and told the little hare his sad tale.

"The woman you seek is in the city beyond. I cannot go there, but I know of something that will help you on your way, for you must have clothes in place of your rags and food to restore your strength. Come with me."

So the Star Child went with the hare who led him to the hollow of a great oak tree and inside was a piece of white gold.

"You have repaid me a hundred times for the service I performed," exclaimed the Star Child.

"No," answered the hare, "I treated you with the same kindness you treated me." Then it ran away swiftly, and the Star Child set off toward the city.

Now at the gate of the city there was seated a leper. Over his face hung a tattered cloth of gray linen and through the eyelets, the Star Child could see his eyes gleaming like red coals. When he saw the Star Child coming, he struck upon a wooden bowl and clattered his bell and called out, "Give me a piece of money, or I must die of hunger. They have thrust me out of the city, and there is none who has pity on me."

"Alas!" cried the Star Child, "I have but one piece of money."

But the leper entreated him and prayed of him, and the Star Child had pity and gave him the piece of white gold.

"Your need is greater than mine," he said, but his heart was heavy as he turned to the gates of the city, for he knew too well how men treat beggars.

But as he passed through the gate, the guards bowed down to him saying, "How beautiful is our king!" causing the Star Child to weep at their mockery. The priests and the high officers of the city ran forth to meet him and said, "You are our king for whom we have been waiting."

"I am no king's son," said the Star Child, "but the son of a beggar woman.

How can you say I am beautiful when you know I am evil to look at?"

One of the guards held up his shield to the Star Child's face and said, "How can my lord say that he is not beautiful?"

The Star Child looked and saw that his face was as it had been and his beauty had come back to him.

The priests and the high officers knelt down and said to him, "It was prophesied of old that on this day should come the king that was to rule over us."

But he said to them, "I am not worthy, for I have denied my mother, nor may I rest until I have found her and known her forgiveness."

And as he spoke he turned his face from them and, lo, amongst the crowd that pressed round the soldiers, he saw the beggar woman who was his mother, and at her side stood the leper who had sat by the side of the road.

A cry of joy broke from his lips. He ran over, and kneeling down he kissed the wounds on his mother's feet and wet them with his tears. He bowed his head in the dust, and sobbing as one whose heart might break he said to her, "Mother, I denied you in my hour of pride. Accept me in the hour of my humility. Mother, I gave you hatred. Can you now give me love?"

The beggar woman put her hand on his head and said to him, "Rise," and the leper put his hand on his head and said to him, "Rise," also.

He rose up from his knees and looked at them and saw they were a king and queen.

The queen said, "This is your father to whom you gave your wealth."

The king said, "This is your mother whose feet you washed with your tears."

And they fell on his neck and kissed him and brought him into the palace. They clothed him in a golden cloak and set the crown upon his head and the scepter in his hand that he might rule over the kingdom.

Much justice and mercy did he show to all and to the woodcutter sent many rich gifts. Nor would he suffer any to be cruel to bird or beast, but taught love and loving-kindness and charity. And to the poor he gave bread, and to the naked clothes, and there was peace and plenty in the land.

~from Oscar Wilde

One Hair
from a True Sinner

In the garden all the apple trees were blooming. Ducklings waddled over the yard, the fields of grain were green, and everywhere the sound of birds singing could be heard. The minister's daughter — his only child and relation — lay on her back, breathing in the scented air and listening to the jubilant songs of the birds. Judging from their chorus, the day must have been a high holiday; and this was not altogether wrong, for it was Sunday. As the bells in the church tower pealed, the girl sat up suddenly and brushed off her skirt. Then she ran to join the others on their way to church.

"How good and kind God is to people!" thought the young woman as she greeted her neighbors.

But inside the church the minister stood in the pulpit preaching loudly and angrily about the impious and ungrateful behavior of human beings. He said that God would punish them: all who had been evil would burn forever in the flames of hell. Their suffering would never end; eternal fires would roast them.

It was horrible to listen to. And he spoke so well, so convincingly. And what made it all the worse was that the minister spoke from his heart. He believed all that he said. The whole congregation was frightened and horrified, although each of the little flowers outside was preaching a very different sermon from the minister's.

Later that evening, just before bedtime, the minister noticed that his

daughter looked very sad. She was sitting in a chair, staring thoughtfully down at her hands.

"What ails you?" he asked.

"What ails me?" repeated his child and smiled forlornly. "I cannot understand your sermon, Father, that is what is the matter with me. No matter how much I add and subtract, I do not get the same sum as you do. You say that evil people are sinners and will burn in hell eternally; how terribly, terribly long that is. But I, too, am a sinner, Father. Just this morning on the way to church, instead of arriving early and sweeping the pews, I lay in the apple orchard gazing up at the light that filtered through the leaves.

"What will God do with me now? I am only a poor sinful human being and yet I cannot bear to think that even the worst sinner in the whole world should burn eternally. How then do you think that God could bear it — he that is infinitely good and knows how we are tempted? I cannot imagine it, even though you have told me that it is true."

It was fall, and the leaves had fallen from the trees. The minister sat by a dying child's bed. She was his daughter.

"If anyone deserved God's grace it is you, and peacefully you shall sleep in your grave," he mumbled. The child died and he closed her eyes and folded her hands as though in prayer. Then he sang a psalm and prayed.

She was carried to her grave, and two tears ran down the cheeks of the earnest father. His home was silent and still. There was no sunshine there, for she whom he loved had died.

In the middle of the night, a whiff of cold air blew across the minister's face and woke him. It was as if the room were filled with moonshine, but the moon was not yet up. A pale figure stood by his bed. It was the ghost of his daughter. She looked so sorrowfully at him that the minister felt she must want to ask him something.

He sat up in bed and stretched his arms out toward her. "Have you not found peace in your grave? Do you suffer? You, the most innocent, the kindest of children?"

The specter bent her head to answer, yes, and placed her hand upon her breast.

"Can I help you obtain peace?" whispered the minister.

"Yes," answered the poor girl. "I must get a hair, just one hair, from the head of a sinner who is to burn eternally in hell."

"That I will do," the minister cried eagerly. "It will be so easy if that is all you require to release you from your pain. You, who were so good."

"Then follow me," commanded the ghost. "For it has been granted you that you can fly as swiftly as your thoughts to wherever you desire to go. I shall accompany you, but before the cock crows you must have found one person who is by God condemned to the eternal fires."

Quickly, carried by thought, they stood in the doorway of a rich man's house.

"In there, yes, in there. Oh, if I were only sure," mumbled the minister as they looked in at broad stairs leading up to a great ballroom. The sound of dance music could be heard all the way down in the street. A servant carrying a cane with a gold knob on its end barred the entrance to those who were not invited.

"Our ball is as elegant as a king's," he said as he looked at the mob that had gathered outside, and on the servant's face the minister saw contempt for those in the street.

"Pride," whispered the ghost. "Pride is a mortal sin. Take the hair from him!"

"Him?" The rector shook his head. "He is only a fool, a clown. He will not

be punished in the eternal fires."

Next they flew to the bare rooms of a miser, where the old man lay, freezing and hungry, on a rickety bed. The miser was so miserable, and yet his thoughts clung to his gold. They saw him rise and throw off his threadbare covering. With feverish, trembling hands he removed a stone in the wall, and from the hole there he took out a stocking filled with gold coins. His cold hands shook as he counted and recounted every coin.

"Greed," whispered the ghost. "Greed is a mortal sin. Let me have a hair from his head."

"But he is sick!" argued the minister. "It is insanity, hopeless, meaningless insanity. What fears, what evil dreams must he not experience?"

They fled, and soon they stood in the large cell of a prison where the criminals slept, side by side, on their plank beds. Like a wild animal, one of them screamed in his sleep.

"Shut up, you ox, and sleep!" muttered his neighbor. "You wake me every night."

"Every night," repeated the man who had screamed. "Yes, every night I hear it howl, and it comes to try to strangle me. My evil temper has led me to do wrong, and twice before have I been inside these walls. But have I not been punished?

"To one crime I have not confessed, though, and this has been my undoing. It happened on the day when I was released from prison and anger boiled within me. I took a match and struck it against the wall of a cottage. Without thought, I tossed it upon the thatched roof which was soon ablaze. The house burned, for the fire had a temper like mine. I helped save the furniture and got the horses out. No living thing, man or beast, lost its life, except for an old dog who was chained. I forgot him. One could hear him howling amid the flames.

"That howling beast still visits every time I want to sleep, and if I finally close my eyes, then the dog comes, big and furry, and lies down upon my chest until I suffocate. Listen to me! You who sleep all night while I only rest for minutes, listen!"

In fury, the man threw himself upon his comrade and hit his face as hard as he could.

"Angry Lars has gone mad again!" shouted the other criminals as they jumped out of bed and threw themselves upon the furious man. They wrestled with him, forced his head down between his legs, and tied him up. His eyes were bloodshot, and he could hardly breathe.

"You will kill him!" shouted the minister. "Poor unfortunate!" He stretched out his arm to protect the poor sinner who had suffered so.

As the night passed the minister and his daughter's ghost flew through the halls of the rich and the hovels of the poor. Envy, greed, lust — all the mortal sins they saw. An angel read out both the crimes and what could be said in each person's defense. Often that was not much, but God, who can read our hearts and knows all, knows too of all the evil that tempts us both from within and without. He is all mercy, all love.

The minister's hand shook. He did not dare raise it to tear a hair from the head of a sinner. And then the cock crowed!

"Have pity, God," the minister begged, "and give her peace in her grave that I could not bring her."

"Oh, but you have," said the ghost of his daughter. "For it was your harsh words, your judgment over God and his creation, that made me come tonight. Did you not this night learn that even in the most evil person there is a godly part?"

The minister began to cry, and his tears were the waters of grace.

Someone pressed a kiss on the minister's mouth, and he opened his eyes. The sun was shining into the room. There stood his daughter alive and smiling down at him. She had just awakened him from a dream that God had sent him.

~ from Hans Christian Andersen

The Girl Who Caused the Stars to Weep

Once, long ago, a woodcutter lived with his wife and child in a great pine forest. The child spent her time traveling among the villages that lay at the edge of the woods. There she collected any garments in need of mending, for her mother was a talented seamstress. In this way the child was raised as much by the animals and birds of the forest as by her mother and father. She grew up strange to the ways of man but closer to God whose greatness she witnessed with every step she took. The smooth speckled oval of a quail's egg, the carefully rolled tendrils of a young fern, and the warbling music of the forest thrush were all things of great beauty that God created.

The children in the villages laughed at her for her clothes were worn and thin, and her bonnet and apron, though well turned out, were made from scraps of cloth her mother had collected. Her hair was often full of leaves and twigs from the crowns and necklaces she fashioned as she walked.

But the elders of the village kept the children in check for there was something strange about the child that could not be explained, and they did not wish their children to come to any harm by her.

More than once, some unlucky villager found himself deep in the woods as darkness overtook the forest. Having set his mind upon wolves and bears and other ominous forest creatures, he'd been tempted in the direction of a shining light in the hope of finding a peasant's cottage where he might stay the night.

Instead, he came upon the child, who, too tired to go on, had lain down to sleep on a bed of pine needles. From her emanated the light of a hundred torches, and if the wayward hunter or peddler had courage to stay nearby he was safe and warm until the morning light.

Once the girl was away for several days. When she returned she handed her mother a christening gown.

"How sad I am, Mother," she cried, "for I have been to a village on the other side of the forest where many little children and parents alike have taken ill and died from some strange disease. This gown is but a year old, only now you must make the neck and arms a little bigger so the babe can be buried in it."

Her mother took the cloth that was embroidered at the hem with delicate flowers and gathered her own child into her arms. It was not long after the sewing was completed, however, that the child's mother took ill. Though her daughter gathered for her all the healing herbs of the forest, the woman could not be revived. She died two days later and was buried by the child and her father in a grove of spruce trees. Within a week, the child's father surrendered to the same fate and with help from the village sexton was buried alongside his wife.

Cottages cannot be lent for naught, so the child was turned out to make room for boarders who could pay. The sexton, to whose spade still clung the dirt from her father's grave, tried to make some arrangements for the girl, but none in the village would have her, believing her to be in some way bewitched.

"Do not trouble yourself, sir," the child said, "for I am sure to find a situation in one of the neighboring villages." Carefully she tied the few pennies her mother had laid by into her apron and disappeared down the forest path.

How easy to dismiss an unwanted care! The sexton saw the child but rarely and since she changed little in appearance did not concern himself over her welfare any longer.

In truth, she was so poor that she no longer had a room in which to live nor a bed in which to sleep. Though she traveled far in search of employment, her story had traveled farther. No one was willing to board the child. She had been forsaken by the entire world, but since she was a good and pious child she trusted that the good Lord would look after her.

One evening, she found herself at the outskirts of the village from which she had collected the christening gown. Having eaten nothing the entire day, the poor child was faint with hunger and spent her last penny on a piece of bread.

As she traveled on her way, she met a poor boy, who said, "Ah, give me something to eat. I'm so hungry."

The child handed him her entire piece of bread and said, "May God bless you," and continued on her way.

By the side of the road she spied a fallen sparrow. When she discovered that it was dead, she wrapped it gently in her kerchief and dug a grave for it with her own hands.

After she had gone a little way farther, she met another child who, like herself, had been orphaned. The poor thing had no jacket and was freezing, so she gave him hers. Then the boy brought forward his sister whose own dress lay in tatters over her shoulders.

"You, too, must have something for the cold," said the child tenderly, and she unbuttoned her dress and slipped it over the little girl's shoulders.

Then the boy and his sister began to cry, for the child stood before them in only a thin shirt and night was coming on and it was cold.

"Please, don't grieve on my account," said the child. "I will find shelter in the forest." And she set off on her way. Finally, she reached the forest. It had already become dark and she met yet another child who asked her for a shirt.

The sweet child thought, "It is dark and nobody can see me, so I might as well give this poor soul my shirt. For does not God dress the lilies and the sparrows, too?" So she took off the shirt and gave it away, also.

The stars gazed down at the naked child and wept at her generosity. And their tears were golden coins that fell to the earth around her. Though she had just given away her little shirt, she now had a new one of the finest linen. Within its folds she gathered the gleaming coins and returned to the village where the children lived in such sorrow and took care that none was in want for the rest of her life.

~ *from the Brothers Grimm*

What Men and Women Live By

A cobbler named Simon, and his wife, Katrina, and their children had lodgings with a peasant. They owned neither house nor land. Bread was dear and labor poorly paid, and whatever the cobbler earned went for food.

One day, as the cobbler was returning home, he came to a crossroads by which stood a little chapel. At the entrance sat a man, entirely naked, shivering with cold.

"Shall I go to him, or shall I go on? If I go to him, something unpleasant might happen. Who knows what sort of man he is?" And the cobbler hurried on his way.

But after he traveled a short distance, he came to his senses.

"Simon, what are you doing?" he asked himself. "A man is perishing of cold, and you are so frightened you hurry by? Ah, this is not right." So the cobbler hurried back to the chapel.

The cobbler went up to the young man who suddenly seemed to revive. The man lifted his head and fastened his eyes on the cobbler. And by this glance, the man won the cobbler's heart.

Simon threw down a pair of felt boots he had just collected for repair, took off his belt, laid it on the boots, and pulled off his tunic.

"There's nothing to be said," he exclaimed. "Put these on." The cobbler put his hand under the man's elbow and lifted him up. The man looked

affectionately at Simon, but he did not say a word.

"Why don't you say something? We can't spend the winter here. We must get to shelter. Lean on my stick here," the cobbler said gruffly. And the man did as he was told.

The cobbler's wife was also speechless when they arrived home.

"He has gone and drunk up his money," Katrina thought to herself. "He has been on a spree with this miserable beggar, and, worse than all, he has brought him home!"

As she fixed her gaze upon the man, the man froze. He did not raise his eyes.

And Katrina thought, "He is not a good man. His conscience bothers him."

"Well," said Simon. "Can't you get us something to eat?"

"How shall I feed this beggar when our money has been squandered?" Katrina shouted.

Simon took his wife gently by the shoulders. "Can it be, Katrina, that God is not in you? I found this man freezing with cold at the entrance to the chapel in the woods."

Katrina looked deeply into her husband's eyes and knew what he told her was true. She set the last half loaf in the house before the stranger. Simon cut the bread and crumbled it into the bowl, and they began to eat their supper. Katrina sat at the end of the table, leaned on her hand, and gazed at the stranger. She began to feel sorry for him.

Suddenly, the stranger brightened up, ceased to frown, lifted his eyes to Katrina, and smiled. After they finished supper, she put away the dishes and took from the window an old shirt of Simon's she had been patching. She found a pair of pants and these she gave the man also.

"Well," said Simon. "If you aren't willing to tell about yourself that is your own affair. But the belly asks for bread, and you must earn a living. What do you know how to do?"

"There is nothing that I know how to do."

"A man can learn anything he has a mind to. If you're willing to work, I will keep you."

Simon threaded a needle. The stranger looked, then threaded his own needle expertly. Simon showed him how to make a welt. The stranger did this also. Whatever part of work Simon showed him he imitated and soon learned Simon's trade better than the cobbler himself.

Day after day, week after week rolled by for a whole year. The fame of Simon's apprentice went abroad, and the cobbler prospered. The stranger worked without relaxation and spoke only when necessary. He smiled but once, on that first evening, when Katrina fed him.

One winter's day, a grand sleigh drew up outside Simon's cottage. Soon a robust nobleman in a fur coat entered the cottage.

"Bring me the leather, Fedka," the nobleman shouted to his footman. "Now listen, shoemaker, do you see this leather? It's fine German leather. It cost me twenty rubles. Can you make me a pair of boots out of this leather that will not rip or lose shape for one year?"

Simon hesitated. He glanced at the stranger who stood staring at a point just beyond the giant nobleman. The stranger stared, then suddenly smiled, as if he saw someone or something.

Simon took it as a sign. He cleared his throat. "With such fine leather I am sure I can."

"Then take the measure!" The nobleman shouted and held out his leg to be fitted.

When Simon and the stranger were alone, Simon began to fret: "We must not make any blunder. Your eye has become quicker than mine. You will make the boots." And he handed the stranger the measure and left the cottage to deliver a pair of shoes.

But when Katrina returned to the work room she saw the stranger cutting the leather not for a pair of thick-soled boots, but in a rounded manner, as if for slippers. By the time Simon had returned, the slippers were finished. The shoemaker groaned, "You have ruined me! You know the nobleman ordered boots, and what have you made?"

At that moment, a knock on the door was followed by the nobleman's footman peering anxiously into the cobbler's hut.

"My mistress sent me about the boots. You see, the baron needs the boots no longer for he died on the return journey. Just like that." The man was evidently quite startled for he kept repeating, "Just like that. We went to help him out of the sleigh, and he had fallen over like a bag, stone dead. Just like that. Now, mistress wonders if you could make a pair of slippers for the corpse out of that leather as soon as possible."

To the footman's astonishment, Simon handed over the slippers for his master's corpse.

Still another year, then two more passed by, and the stranger had been living with Simon and Katrina for five years. He lived just the same way as before. He kept his own counsel, never went anywhere, and was seen to smile only twice.

One day one of the children shouted from the doorway, "Father, look! A merchant's wife is coming to the door with two little girls. One is a cripple. Father, look!"

Simon looked out his window and saw a woman coming toward him. She was neatly dressed and had two little girls by the hand who looked so alike it was hard to tell them apart, except that one child limped as she walked.

"These little girls need goatskin shoes for the spring," explained the woman. Simon glanced at the stranger who had thrown down his work and was sitting with his eyes fastened on the little girls. Simon could not understand why the stranger gazed at them so intently. Yes, they were pretty. They dressed fashionably, were plump and rosy, and their dark eyes shone.

"Please take two measures," the woman was saying. Make one little shoe for the twisted foot, and three from the well one. Their feet are alike. They are twins."

Simon took his tape and said, "How did this happen to her? Was she born so?"

"No. Her mother crushed it."

"Then you aren't their mother? You take such good care of them."

"Why shouldn't I? I nursed them at my own breast. I had a baby of my own, but God took him when he was but three years old."

Simon nodded, and the woman told him her story.

"Six years ago, these little ones were left orphans in one week. Their father, a woodcutter, was pinned under a falling tree, and their mother died in childbirth. They were poor, and she was alone at the birth. I came early one morning to look in on my neighbor and found the poor thing dead and cold. She must have rolled over on the little girl and crushed her foot. I was the only one with a child at the time, and so I took them in. I had three children at the breast! But I was young and strong, and God let me nurse all three."

Katrina sighed and said, "The old saw isn't far wrong. One can live without father or mother, but without God one cannot live."

While they were talking, a flash of light seemed to radiate from that corner of the cottage where the stranger was sitting. He sat with his hands folded in his lap, and he was smiling.

The woman went away, and the stranger arose from the bench and laid down his work.

"Farewell, friends. God calls me."

Simon realized that it was from the stranger that the light flashed and he bowed low before him and said, "I see you are not a mere man, and I have no right to detain you or ask you questions. But if you please, will you tell me why you smiled these three times? The first was when my wife had pity on you and fed you. The second time was when the baron ordered the boots. The third time in five years was just now when the woman brought her two little girls."

"It was required of me to learn three of God's truths," the stranger replied quietly.

And Simon said, "Please, what were these truths of God, that I might know them?"

"I was an angel in heaven, and the Lord sent me to retrieve the soul of a certain woman. I flew down to earth and saw the woman lying alone. She had just given birth to two little girls.

"And when the woman saw that God had sent me, she begged for mercy. I put the children at her breast and returned to God. And the Lord said, 'Go and take the mother's soul and learn three lessons before you return to heaven. First you shall learn what is in men and women; next, what is not given to them; and third, what they live by.'

"That first night when you reminded your wife of God, I saw a change in her, and she looked kindly on me. I learned then what is in men and women alike. It is love. When the rich nobleman arrived at your door, I perceived the Angel of Death beside him. It was then I learned what is not given; that is, the knowledge of what lies ahead. He planned for a year, but he had only one hour to live. At this realization, I smiled a second time.

"Today I have learned the third lesson. I recognized the little ones. Their mother entreated me on their behalf, saying they could not live without her. But in this woman, who caressed and cared for children who were not her own, I saw the Living God and came to know what men and women live by. I knew God had revealed to me the last truth, and I smiled a third time.

Then the angel's body became apparent, and he was clad in light so bright the eyes could not look upon him. His voice proceeded not from him, but as from heaven.

"I have now learned that it is only in appearance that people are kept alive through care for themselves, but that in reality they are kept alive through love. Those who dwell in love dwell in God and God in them, for God is love."

And the angel sang a hymn of praise to God. The ceiling parted and wings appeared on the angel's shoulders, and he soared to heaven.

When Simon opened his eyes, the cottage was the same as it had ever been, and there was no one in it, save himself and his family.

~from Count Leo Tolstoy

The Princess Who Never Smiled

When you come to think of it, how great is God's world! Rich people live in it, and poor people live in it. All of them have room to live, and the Lord keeps watch over all.

In a royal palace, in a princely castle, in a lofty apartment, there lived the glorious Princess Who Never Smiled. What a life she had, what plenty, what luxury! She had a great deal of everything. She had everything her heart desired. Yet she never smiled, and she never laughed. It was as though her heart did not delight in anything.

The king was distressed when he looked at his sorrowful daughter. He opened his royal palace to any man who wished to be his guest.

"Let them try," said he, "to divert the Princess Who Never Smiled. He who succeeds shall take her to be his wife."

No sooner was the proclamation given than people began to throng the royal gate. They came from all sides, princes and dukes, knights and noblemen, people of rank and commoners alike. Feasts were held, wine flowed, dancing and merrymaking of all manner and description rang forth. But still the princess did not smile.

At the other end of town in a corner of his own, there lived an honest worker. In the morning he swept the courtyard. In the evening he grazed the cattle. Indeed, he worked without ceasing. His master, a rich and righteous man, paid him a proper wage. At the end of the year he put a bag of money on the table and said to the worker, "Take as much as you want." And then he went out of the room.

The poor man approached the table. That he was troubled by something was plain to see. He touched the great bag of money, all the while thinking, "How shall I avoid sinning against the Lord by taking too much for my work?" After a long while, he took only one coin and left the room.

Just then, he felt a strange thirst come over him, and with the coin pressed tightly in his fist he went to the well to take a drink of water. As he stooped over the cool water, the coin fell out of his hand and sank to the bottom of the well.

The poor fellow was left with nothing. Another in his place would have wept, grieved, and wrung his hands in despair, but not this man.

"God sends us everything," he said. "The Lord knows what to give to whom. Some he endows generously with money, from others he takes the last penny." The man thought at length about his year of work. Had he been careless? Had he worked badly? He vowed then and there to give twice the effort that he had the year before. So he set his mind to work, and his fingers flew more nimbly than fire itself.

Another year went by, and his master again put a bag of money on the table, telling him, "Take as much as your heart desires." Again he left the room. Again the poor man did not want to displease God and take too much for work. He took a coin, went to drink at the well, and dropped his coin. Again it sank. Again he examined his conduct and set to work even more feverishly, hardly eating by day, hardly resting by night.

And lo and behold, while other people's grain withered, his master's thrived. While other people's cattle collapsed from exhaustion, his master's capered in the street. Other people's horses had to be dragged uphill, his master's had to be held back.

The master knew to whom he owed all this. When the term was completed and the third year had passed, he put a pile of money on the table, saying, "Take, little worker, take as much as your heart desires. Yours was the labor; yours is the money." And he left the room.

Again the worker took only one coin and went to the well to drink water. This time he gripped his coin so tightly in his fist that he could not possibly lose it. But as he drank, he felt the metal yield to something soft in his palm and when he opened up his hand, he held not a gold coin, but a sheaf of wheat. And while he was pondering this, he saw the coins he had previously dropped in the well rise to the surface. As he scooped them out, they too changed into something else. The first became a bit of dung; the second a dead fly. The man beheld the treasures in his palm. He scratched his head and stroked his beard. Then he laughed a great hearty laugh and deposited the sheaf of wheat, the bit of dung, and the dead fly into his pocket.

"I see that God has rewarded me now for my labors," he said. "It is high time for me to see the wide world and to know people."

So he set off in the direction of his feet and soon came to a great field where a mouse ran up to him and stopped, quite out of breath. "My dear comrade," he panted. "Please give me your sheaf of wheat. I will be useful to you someday."

"Gladly, little friend," replied the man, and he gave the mouse his sheaf of wheat. The man continued on his way until he came to a great forest. There in his path was a large beetle peering up at him.

"My dear comrade," said the beetle in a low dignified voice. "Be so kind as to give me that bit of dung in your pocket. I am sure to be useful to you someday."

"With pleasure," said the man, who had never seen such a dignified dung beetle in all his life.

Finally, he came to a great river. As he swam across, he was approached by a large catfish with quivery whiskers, who said, "Be so good as to let me have that little fly in your pocket, comrade. I am sure to be of some use to you someday."

"The fly is yours," said the man, tossing it into the gaping mouth of the catfish.

The man pulled himself onto the bank, water streaming from his empty pockets. Though some would ponder this strange turn of events, the young man simply turned his face toward the sun and gave thanks to God for crossing the swift river safely.

There in the distance was a gleaming tower that shone like a jeweled crown in the sun. He followed the dancing lights to a great city. Never before had the young man seen so many people, so many doors! The worker looked at everything with awe. He followed the cobbled streets through markets and busy lanes, but he did not know where to go. At length he found himself in the courtyard of the Princess Who Never Smiled.

There she sat in the window, dressed splendidly in silver and gold, looking straight at him, and wearing her most sorrowful expression.

Where would he hide? The young man meant to search for a place to conceal himself, but he could not take his eyes from the sad and lovely princess. He stood transfixed, unable to move, as throngs of people conducted their business all around him. There he stood for what seemed like hours, until his strength failed him and he fainted and he fell, face down in the mud.

As though from nowhere came the catfish with the great quivery whiskers, standing upright on his tail fins and delicately picking his way through the mud. He was followed closely by the dung beetle and the mouse.

All of them gathered around the unfortunate man and set to work. The little mouse removed his coat, the beetle cleaned the mud from his boots, and the catfish chased the flies away.

The Princess Who Never Smiled watched and watched their antics until

finally she burst out laughing.

The king's steps rang out in the hallway. "Who, I ask, who has cheered my daughter?"

"It was I," said the duke.

"I am responsible," said the knight.

"No," said the Princess Who Never Smiled. "It was this man," and she pointed out the window to the honest young worker. The crowd that had gathered outside ushered the young man into the palace. The king's servants brushed his hair until it shone and exchanged his clothes for princely garments.

When he stood before the king, the honest worker was transformed into a handsome youth.

The king kept his royal promise, and with permission from the princess he wed the two that very day and gave them half his kingdom, thinking all the while to himself that the sound of his daughter's joyful laughter was well worth the price.

~from Aleksandr Afanas'ev

The Finch's Flight

Once, in the old, old days, there was a finch who was wise enough to nest in the linden tree that grew in the heart of a convent garden. Wise enough? No doubt the idea was an inspiration from on high. God watches over all things, even the life of a finch.

There was yet another who took refuge within the convent walls. That was the gravedigger's son. By bending and turning the branches in the thick hedge, the child fashioned for himself a kind of nest that kept out the worst of the rain and snow and bitter winds.

The poor thing needed refuge. Small for his age and weak from birth, he was of little use to his father, who when he wasn't digging or drinking was often heard cursing the child and beating him with the broken handle of a spade.

Without consulting one another, the nuns kept the child's hiding place a secret and did not turn him out. When they scattered crumbs for the birds, they often dropped half a loaf onto the stump of the great fir that had been struck by lightning the year before. More than likely, it contained a fat slice of cheese or beef tucked inside as well.

Birds and mice and other little creatures were the child's only friends. So quiet and gentle was he that they soon lost their fear of him. Just as the young finch claimed the garden for her own, she also claimed the child, eating crumbs straight from his hand or perching on his shoulder as he walked about the

garden and sang sweetly in harmony with the nuns whose voices rose in prayer.

The same two words kept coming back. Eight times a day, from morning to noon to setting sun, perched on the boy's shoulder the little finch heard them, listened again, then tried them out with her own little bird throat.

It was May, Mary's month, when narcissus bloom in the high meadows, the flowers they call the White Gloves of Our Lady. The leaves swayed, and the sunbeams paused to dance with them on their journey to the earth. There in the green moving light and the gentle breezes the finch repeated those two words over and over — "Ave Maria! Ave Maria!"

The convent stood under steep forested slopes and towering spires of rock. Beneath a spur of the mountains, the child would often stand mesmerized at the beauty that surrounded him. His faint heart was not long for this world, he knew, so he must drink in the wonder of creation in great gulps.

The light breezes of spring gave way to a long sultry summer. Whenever the boy could he stole away to his nest in the brambled hedge, and the finch greeted him with her song of joy.

In the fall the child set off to gather once again the soft pine needles with which he lined his nest to keep out the worst of the bitter winter winds. The finch followed him into those piney stony wilds, darting through the trees and keeping a watchful eye on the child.

Suddenly, the little bird felt a presence hovering above her under the clouds. Crying out, she used all the speed in her wings to race toward the convent roof and its home.

But a hawk's eyes are piercing. The one slowly circling up there, round and round in the streaming clouds and wind, stopped like a spider hanging from its thread. The white bands on the finch's wings had given her away. With an eerie cry the hawk soared down toward the fleeing finch.

Helpless from below, the child watched the chase, then set off in the same direction at a pace much faster than his poor heart could accommodate.

The hawk swooped down and gripped the finch in its talons.

Nearly fainting, the little bird cried out. She cried out the two words that had so gotten into her head that she had said them over and over all the long day — "Ave Maria, Ave Maria."

So great is the power of Mary that her name alone, just one call to Our Lady, loosened the hawk's grip. Up again into the clouds the hawk flew, not daring now to touch its prey.

The bird met the boy in the garden, dove under his thin shirt in terror, and was still. The child was strangely pale. He walked slowly to the hollow in the hedge and climbed into it. There he lay, curled up like a baby, the heat of his body reviving the stricken bird.

When nightfall came the bird crept out and flew back to her nest in the linden tree, but the boy did not move.

A light snow fell that evening, dusting the ground and the branches with a dry white powder. Flakes settled on the child's lashes and nose, but he did not stir.

The nuns found him under a glittering cover of snow the next morning and carried his frail body to the chapel. They sent a message to his father to come and to bring a small pine box for the body of his child. Aside from the nuns, only one joined the funeral party. That was a charwoman from the village who had pitied him.

The boy's father waited outside the church, his spade in hand. He waited for the funeral to be over so that he might bury his only son.

But God would not return the child to his father, even in death. The doors of the little chapel blew open, and a crisp breeze passed through the church, carrying with it the sound of wings beating the air. A flock of birds swept in through the tall arched entry and alighted on the casket. Finches every one, they sang out in glory to Mary, Mother of All, entreating her to take this poor child home to be with her own.

Suddenly, in their midst appeared a glossy white dove with glittering eyes whose call was the voice of a child in song. Together with the finches, rising in chorus, the church resounded with the anthem — "Ave Maria, Ave Maria!"

The dove unfurled wings that shone like beaten gold and slowly ascended to the ceiling of the chapel. There he hovered, bathing the room in sunlight with his wondrous feathers. Then steeply he dove and joined together with the other smaller birds as they winged their way out of the church and into the glowing air.

The nuns streamed through the chapel doors to watch the procession as it climbed to the spires of the village church and alighted there. These two flew on alone, the wondrous dove with the little finch by his side, up, up, up, higher and higher, to their home in the shining heavens.

~from Henri Pourrat

Author's Note

The tales collected here have ancestors that date back to the 14th and 15th centuries. As Christianity spread through western and eastern Europe, religious motifs were woven into traditional oral tales. Eventually these tales were collected and written down. I have drawn from a variety of sources to retell the stories you've read here. In retelling the stories, I have edited, changed, and embellished them. Some bear only a passing likeness to the tales that first inspired them. I have set "The Shepherd's Prayer" in the desert southwest, for example. Others I've condensed to be read in one sitting. The following are some notes on the sources of my tales, so that if you enjoy them you may look up the authors and read others of their stories.

"The Shepherd's Prayer" is built from a brief folktale entitled "The Prayer of the Shepherd" that can be found in *Mimekor Yisrael: Classic Jewish Folktales, Volume III*, collected by Micha Joseph bin Gorion.

"Péquelé" is a beautiful tale from *Le Tresor des Contes* (*A Treasury of Tales*), a seven-volume collection of tales by the French folktale writer Henri Pourrat.

"The Angel" comes from a little booklet entitled *New Fairy Tales* by Hans Christian Andersen, originally published in 1845.

"Where Love Is, God Is Also" is drawn from a story by Count Leo Tolstoy originally published in 1885. This story has been retold for children under the title "Martin the Shoemaker" and as a Christmas story in "The Shoemaker's Dream."

"The Star Child" is an abbreviated version of Oscar Wilde's story of the same name, originally published in his collection called *The House of Pomegranates* in 1892.

"One Hair from a True Sinner" was originally titled "A Story" and collected in a short volume of tales, *In Sweden*, written by Hans Christian Andersen, first published in 1851.

"The Girl Who Caused the Stars to Weep" comes from a very brief story related by the Brothers Grimm, originally titled "The Star Coins," published in 1812.

"What Men and Women Live By" is adapted from a much longer story by Count Leo Tolstoy, originally published in 1881.

"The Princess Who Never Smiled" was originally collected and rewritten by Aleksandr Afanas'ev, considered by many to be the Russian counterpart to the Brothers Grimm.

"The Finch's Flight" was originally titled "A Finch in May" and was built from a short piece by Henri Pourrat, originally published in *Le Tresor des Contes* (*A Treasury of Tales*).